50 Science Things to Make & Do

Written by Georgina Andrews and Kate Knighton
Designed & illustrated by
Zöe Wray, Tom Lalonde, Katie Lovell and Stella Baggott
Photography by Howard Allman
Consultants: Dr. Catherine Cooper and Liz Lander,
Science Curriculum Coordinator, Roehampton University

Contents

Shadow show   8

Catch the birdie   10

Cooking in the Sun   12

Wind power   14

Caterpillar search   16

Climbing ink   18

Making gloop   20

Chiming fork   22

Stable structures   24

Water power   26

Hovering butterfly   28

Bug watch   30

Jumping pepper   32

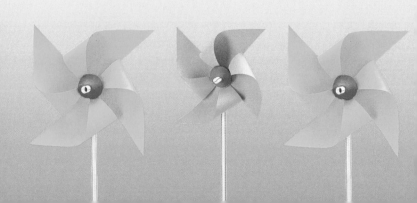

Falling orange	34
Oily mixtures	36
Elastic band guitar	38
Elastic band paddle boat	40
Butterfly feeder	42
Kaleidoscope	44
Be a snake charmer	46
Balancing acrobats	48
Milk shapes	50
Foaming monster	52
Fire a balloon rocket	54
Sinking diver	56

Seeing DNA	58
Paper planes	60
Meringue science	62
Making butter	64
Fruity ice slush	66
Floating flowers	68
Make a wormery	70
Team trail	72
Speedy shoots	74
Indicator paper	76
Surface tension	78
Flick book	80
Bottle flute	82

Spider slider	84
Words and pictures	86
Tricky pictures	88
Name that face	90
Pinhole projector	92
What grows best?	94
Wind vane	96
Hanging crystals	98
Paper compass	100
Rainbow patterns	102
Quacking duck vibrations	104
Salt and candy crystals	106
Index	108

Shadow show

Perform a show for your
friends, using light
and shadows.

Use dark paint.

1. Paint some tree trunks and leaves on a big piece of white paper. Add some grass and flowers at the bottom.

2. To make a crocodile puppet, draw a body shape on a piece of cardboard. Then add jaws and a tail.

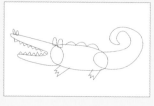

3. Draw bumps for eyes and nostrils, and a few bumps along its back. Add some sharp teeth and legs.

4. Cut around it. Tape a straw to its body, like this. You can make other animal puppets in the same way.

The paper should touch the floor.

5. Use masking tape to attach the screen between two chairs, with the painted side facing the front.

6. Darken the room. Put a lamp behind the chairs. Switch on the lamp and shine it on the screen.

The shadow will fall on the paper.

7. Sit behind the chairs and the screen. Hold your puppet by the straw, so that it's nearly touching the paper.

8. Move your puppet to make it perform. The audience will see the puppet's shadow on the screen.

What's going on?

Light from the lamp passes through the unpainted areas of the screen. But the puppet blocks the light, casting a shadow onto the screen.

The audience can see the shadow from this side.

Catch the birdie

Try this activity to find out how your brain can trick your eyes.

1. Make two circles on a piece of thin white card, by drawing around a mug twice. Then cut them out.

Make the cage a bit bigger than the bird.

2. Draw a bird on one circle and a cage on the other. Turn the cage upside down. Glue them together back to back.

3. Use a hole puncher to make two holes on either side of the cage. Cut two pieces of string as long as your arm.

4. Thread a piece of string through one pair of holes, like this. Knot the ends. Do the same on the other side.

Keep swinging the disc until all the string is twisted.

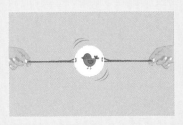

5. Hold the knots so that the circle hangs down. Flip the circle over and around until the string is twisted up tightly.

6. Now, with both hands, pull the string tight. This makes the circle spin around really fast. What can you see?

What's going on?

As the circle spins, your eyes see one picture after the other. The pictures come around so fast that your brain can't separate them. Instead, it merges the two. So you see one picture — of the bird caught inside the cage.

Cooking in the Sun

Choose a sunny day to discover
how you can trap the Sun's heat.

1. Line a large bowl with kitchen foil. Then press a piece of poster tack down in the middle of the bowl.

2. Put a marshmallow on the end of a cocktail stick. Push the other end of the cocktail stick into the poster tack.

3. Cover the top of the bowl with clear food wrap. Then put the bowl outside in a sunny place.

4. Use stones to prop up the bowl. Position it so that the inside is facing the Sun. Leave it for about 15 minutes.

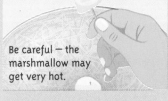

Be careful — the marshmallow may get very hot.

5. The marshmallow should start to melt. If it hasn't, leave it for another 15 minutes and check again.

What's going on?

The food wrap lets sunlight into the bowl and traps heat from the Sun. The foil reflects the light and heat around the bowl and onto the marshmallow. This heats it up. Because the air in the bowl is trapped, it gets even hotter, which also speeds up the cooking.

Wind power

Explore how wind power can provide energy in this experiment.

1. Cut out a square of bright paper, 10 x 10cm (4 x 4in). Cut halfway down from each corner to the middle, like this.

To find the middle point, fold your square in half, then in half again.

2. Fold the corners marked x to the middle and glue them down. The folds should curve and not lie flat.

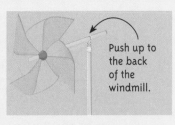

Push up to the back of the windmill.

3. Make a hole in the middle with a pencil and push a straw through. Secure it in position with poster tack.

4. Now tape a paperclip to a second straw, like this. Then push the windmill straw through the paperclip.

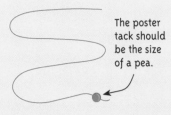

The poster tack should be the size of a pea.

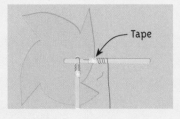

Tape

5. Cut a piece of cotton thread about the length of two straws. Stick a small lump of poster tack to one end.

6. Tape the thread to the windmill straw. Wind the thread around it, leaving some hanging down.

7. Hold the other straw and blow to the side of the windmill. It will spin around, making the thread roll up.

What's going on?

Your breath acts like wind and turns the windmill. This provides energy to pull up your small load of poster tack. Wind farms use much bigger windmills in the same way. The windmills turn machines and supply energy to generators to make electricity.

Caterpillar search

Wait for the summer to try to
hatch your own butterfly.

1. Use a sharp pencil to poke a few holes in the lid of a big, plastic ice-cream tub. Add a few pencil-sized twigs.

2. Look for a caterpillar on a leaf. Put it in the box with the leaf it's on and a few leaves from the same plant.

Don't put the box in direct sunlight.

The fresh leaves must be from the plant you found the caterpillar on.

3. Put the lid on and leave it somewhere warm. Check on your caterpillar every day and put in fresh leaves.

4. After about a couple of weeks the caterpillar should make a protective shell. This looks like a small brown case.

In a warm place, it should hatch between 7-10 days. If it hasn't hatched by then, carefully put it back outside.

5. Now check the box twice a day. As soon as you see a butterfly or a moth, take the box outside and release it.

What's going on?

The twigs provide a place for the caterpillar to spin its protective shell, called a cocoon or chrysalis. It forms this so that it can re-form inside, and emerge as a butterfly or a moth.

Climbing ink

Separate colours in this fascinating activity.

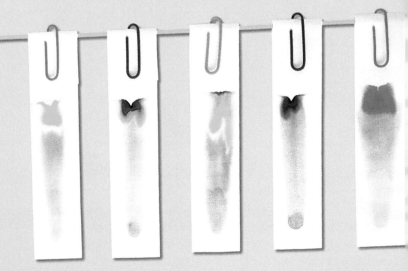

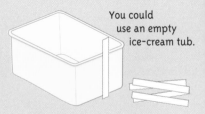

You could use an empty ice-cream tub.

Special equipment

You can buy blotting paper from most stationery stores.

1. Cut some white blotting paper into strips slightly longer than the depth of a large plastic tub.

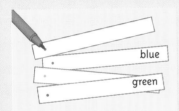

2. Make a dot with a different coloured felt-tip pen a little way up each strip. Write the colour at the top in pencil.

3. Pour just enough water into the tub to cover the bottom. Then tape a piece of string across the top of the tub.

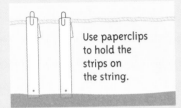

Use paperclips to hold the strips on the string.

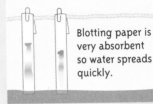

Blotting paper is very absorbent so water spreads quickly.

4. Fold the strips over the string, so that the ends near the dots are in the water, but the dots aren't.

5. The paper will start to soak up water. Lift out the strips after ten minutes. What has happened to the dots?

What's going on?

The ink in most felt-tip pens contains mixtures of different colours. Some colours dissolve more easily in water than others because of the chemicals they contain. These colours spread quickly up the paper. Other colours contain chemicals that don't like water. These colours stick to the paper to avoid the water. So they don't move up the paper as the water spreads.

Brown ink is made up of blue, yellow and pink. You can see this as the colours separate as the ink travels up the paper.

Making gloop

Wear an apron for this messy activity!

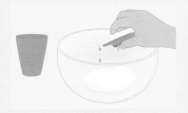

1. To make gloop, put two cups of cornflour into a big bowl. Add a cup of water and two drops of food dye.

2. Mix the cornflour, dye and water with your hands. It will take a few minutes to blend them all together.

3. Roll some of the mixture into a ball between your hands. What happens when you stop rolling?

4. Punch the mixture. How does it feel? Hold it up and let it dribble through your fingers. How does it feel now?

What's going on?

Cornflour is made of lots of long, stringy particles. They don't dissolve in water, but they do spread themselves out. This allows the gloop to act both like a solid and a liquid. When you roll the mixture in your hands or apply pressure to it, the particles join together and the mixture feels solid. But if it is left to rest or is held up and allowed to dribble, the particles slide over each other and it feels like a liquid.

Chiming fork

Try this to find out how sound vibrations work.

Don't tie the thread too tightly around your fingers; it could restrict your blood supply.

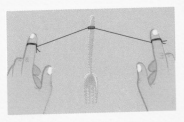

1. Cut a piece of thread as long as your arm. Tie the middle to the end of a fork. Wind the ends around your fingers.

2. Swing the fork so that it knocks gently against the edge of a table. You will hear a dull clink.

3. Now touch your index fingers to the flaps just in front of your ear holes and let the fork hang down.

4. Swing the fork so that it knocks gently against the table again. What do you hear this time?

What's going on?

When the fork hits the table, it vibrates. This makes the air around it vibrate and you hear a dull clink. But it makes the thread vibrate too. When you put your fingers near your ears, you bring the thread closer to the sound sensors in your ears. You can hear the vibrations much more clearly. They now make a clear chiming sound in your ear.

Stable structures

Find out which shapes make the strongest structures.

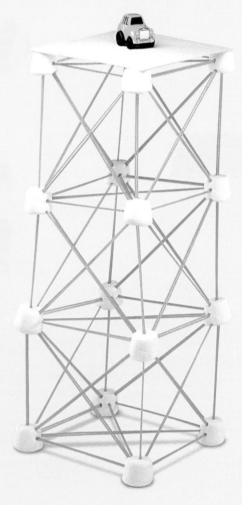

Tower challenge

Be careful! The spaghetti will snap easily.

The diagonals are about two thirds the length of a piece of spaghetti.

1. Use marshmallows and half lengths of uncooked spaghetti to build a cube like this. Does it feel stable?

2. Snap other pieces of spaghetti to make diagonals across each side of the cube. Does it feel more stable now?

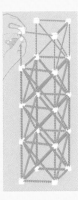

3. Build the tallest tower you can from marshmallows and spaghetti. Put some card on top and see what weight it will support.

Make a pyramid

1. Make a square using half lengths of spaghetti and marshmallows. Add four half lengths to make a pyramid.

What's going on?

Cubes and pyramids make stable structures. Cubes make strong building blocks if they have reinforced diagonals. Pyramids make good structures because they contain triangles, which are one of the strongest shapes.

2. Add more spaghetti to extend your pyramid building like this. How stable does this shape feel?

Water power

Water can provide enough
energy for a power station. Find
out how in this activity.

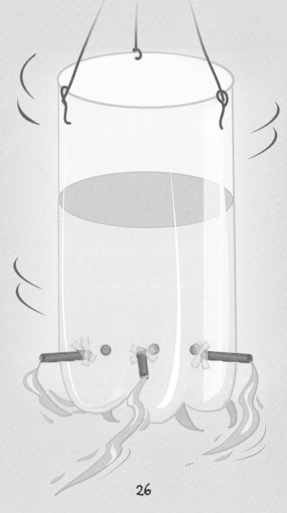

Use a pencil to widen the holes.

1. Cut the top off a large plastic bottle. Use a drawing pin and a pencil to make six holes around the base.

2. Cut a straw into six pieces about 2cm (1in) long. Push them into the holes and secure them with tape.

3. Make three holes at the top of the bottle and tie a piece of string through each hole. Then tie the strings to a fourth piece of string.

The strings should be about the same length.

4. Over the sink or outdoors, pour a jug of water into the bottle. As water pours out of the straws, the bottle will spin around.

What's going on?

The energy from the water pouring out of the holes makes the bottle spin around. Falling water and its energy are used on a much larger scale at hydroelectric power stations. The water turns enormous wheels, called turbines. These drive machines called generators that produce electricity.

27

Hovering butterfly

Use the power of magnetism
to make a butterfly hover.

Special equipment

You can buy strong magnets
from toy or hardware stores.
Don't use fridge magnets, as
they're too weak.

You could
use felt-tip
pens to
decorate
your
butterflies.

1. Lay a shoe box (without a
lid) on its side. Then cut a
piece of thread longer than
the height of the box.

2. Tie a paperclip to one end
of the thread. Cut a butterfly
shape out of tissue paper.
Tape it to the paperclip.

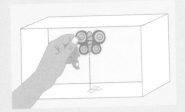

3. Hold the butterfly inside the box, almost touching the top. Pull the thread tight and tape it to the bottom.

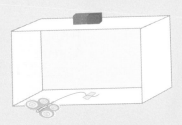

4. Lay a magnet on top of the box, directly above the point where the thread is taped to the bottom.

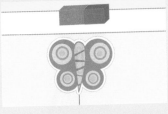

5. Hold the butterfly near the magnet, so the thread is tight. Then let go. The butterfly should hover by itself.

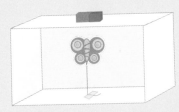

6. Try moving the butterfly further away from the magnet, by shortening the thread. Does it still hover?

What's going on?

Metal paperclips are made from steel which contains iron. The attraction between the magnet and the iron is strong enough for the magnet to pull on the paperclip, even without touching it. The thread stops the paperclip from being pulled onto the magnet. The stronger your magnet, the further away you can move the paperclip and still make it hover.

Bug watch

Search in the soil to find out what's living under your feet.

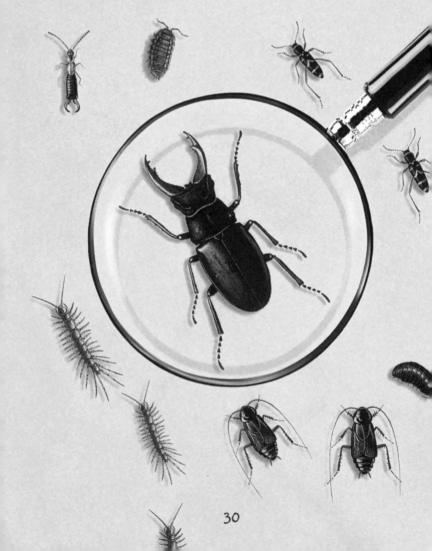

It's easier if you make a hole for the scissors with a drawing pin first.

1. Cut the top third off a large plastic bottle. Take the lid off and put the top part upside down inside the bottom part.

2. Fill the top part with garden soil. Try to use soil with dead leaves on top, as it's a good place to find bugs.

If no bugs fall through, try using soil from another area.

3. Leave it under a lamp for two hours. Some bugs in the soil will burrow down and drop into the bottom part.

4. Do you recognize any of the bugs? Look at them with a magnifying glass. Then return them to the garden.

What's going on?

The bugs burrow down to hide from the heat and light. What you find in the soil will depend on where you live, where you get the soil from, and the time of year. Summer is probably the best time to look. You may find small varieties of bugs, beetles or worms.

Jumping pepper

Investigate the incredible effects
of static electricity in this activity.

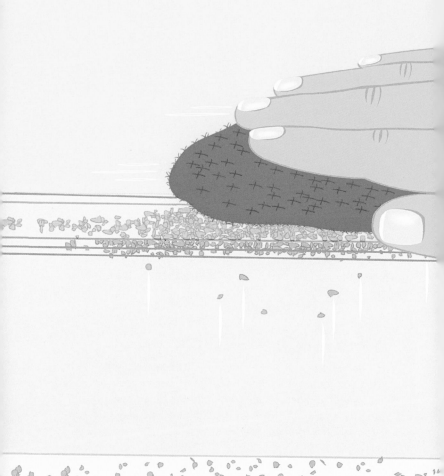

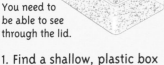

You need to be able to see through the lid.

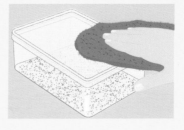

1. Find a shallow, plastic box and sprinkle a thin layer of ground pepper across the bottom of it. Put the lid on.

2. Rub the lid for about half a minute with a woollen scarf or sweater. Stop rubbing and watch the lid.

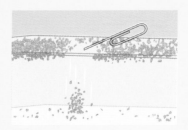

3. Specks of pepper will jump up and stick to the lid. You should see and hear them hitting the top.

4. Unfold a metal paperclip. Touch the lid with one end of it. The pepper will move sideways or drop down.

What's going on?

Rubbing the lid creates a build-up of static electricity, which attracts the pepper. When you touch the lid with the paperclip, the static is transferred to the metal. So the pepper drops down, or is pulled to other parts of the lid that still have static. The static travels through the metal paperclip, then your body and down to the earth, so the paperclip doesn't get a build-up of its own.

Falling orange

Find out about inertia with an
orange, cardboard and a mug.

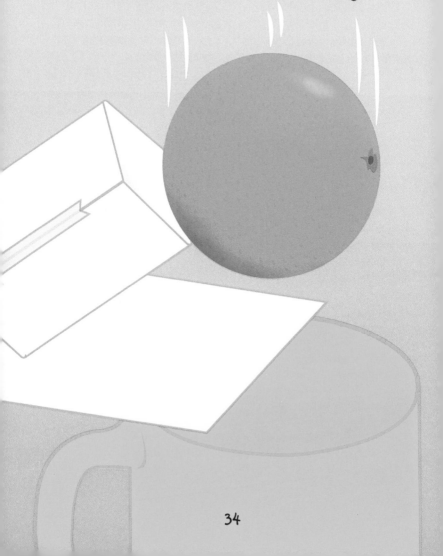

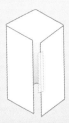 

1. Cut a piece of card 10cm x 8cm (4in x 3in). Fold it into a rectangular column, like this, and tape it together.

2. Lay a postcard on top of a mug. Put the card column on top, so that it's over the middle of the mug.

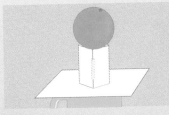 

3. Carefully balance a small orange on top of the column so that the orange is directly above the mug.

4. Pull the postcard away with a sharp tug. The column will fall to the side and the orange will drop into the mug.

What's going on?

The column is light and easily moves sideways when you pull the postcard from underneath. But, the orange is much heavier, so it isn't moved as easily by the same pull – it drops straight down into the mug instead. Scientists call this inertia. Inertia measures how hard it is for a force to move an object. The orange has high inertia, because it's heavier, and the column has low inertia.

Oily mixtures

Can you mix oil and vinegar?
Try it in this tasty experiment.

1. Measure out three tablespoons of vinegar and three tablespoons of olive oil into a clean jar.

2. Notice how the oil floats in a layer on top of the vinegar. This is because the two liquids don't mix.

3. Now screw the lid on the jar tightly and shake the jar for about 30 seconds. How does the mixture change?

4. If you leave the new mixture for a few minutes, the liquids will separate and the layers reappear again.

5. You can use the mixture as a salad dressing. Add a pinch of salt and pepper and shake it again first.

What's going on?

Oil and vinegar don't mix. You can force them to mix temporarily by shaking the jar. But they don't mix together properly. The oil turns into small droplets inside the vinegar. When left to settle, the substances separate again.

Elastic band guitar

Use elastic bands to make different musical notes.

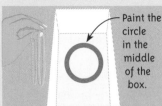

Paint the circle in the middle of the box.

1. Paint a circle in the bottom of a shoe box. Find two elastic bands the same lengths but different thicknesses.

2. Stretch them over the box and pluck each one with your finger. The thinner one makes a higher note.

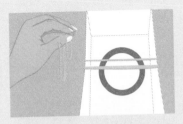

3. Now choose two bands that are the same thickness but different lengths. Which do you think will sound higher?

4. Stretch them over the box and pluck them. The shorter one makes a higher note. Were you right?

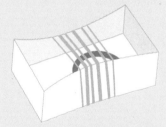

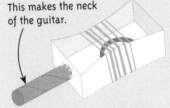

This makes the neck of the guitar.

5. Stretch more elastic bands over the box. Pluck each one and arrange them in order, from the highest to the lowest.

6. Find an inside tube from a roll of paper towels. Attach the tube to one end of your box with sticky tape.

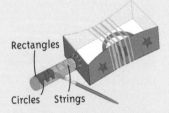

Rectangles

Circles Strings

7. To make it look more like a guitar, you could paint on a rectangle and circles for a guitar head and draw strings.

What's going on?

Thinner elastic bands vibrate more quickly than thicker ones, so they make higher notes. The more an elastic band is stretched, the faster it vibrates. So when shorter ones are stretched, they make higher notes than longer ones.

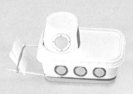
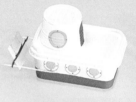
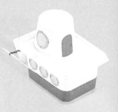

Elastic band paddle boat

Watch elastic energy in action by making this paddle boat.

Keep the lid on.

1. Glue a cocktail stick halfway up one of the long sides of a small, empty margarine tub. It should stick out like this.

2. Glue another stick in the same way to the other side. These will be the supports for your elastic band paddle.

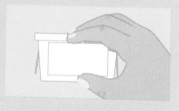

3. From another tub lid, cut a piece the same shape as the end of the boat – but about 1cm (½in) smaller all around.

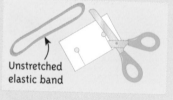

Unstretched elastic band

4. Make two holes in it with a hole puncher. Cut slits into the holes. Find an elastic band as wide as the end of the boat.

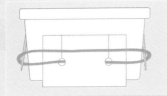

5. Slip the band through the slits into the holes. Then loop the band over the ends of the sticks.

6. To make the captain's "bridge" for your boat, cut a plastic cup in half. Glue it to one end of the box lid.

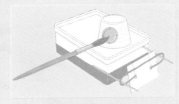

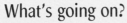
Twist the paddle away from the boat.

7. Paint details on your boat, like this. Then fill a bath or a sink with water and float the boat in it.

8. Wind the paddle until the elastic band is wound tightly. Then let it go. The boat should move through the water.

What's going on?

As you wind up the elastic band, it stretches. When you let go, it unwinds and returns to its original length. The release of this stored energy turns the paddle. This is what moves the boat.

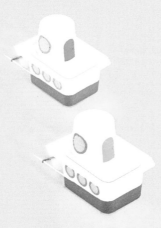

Butterfly feeder

Attract butterflies into your garden with this feeder.

Make knots at each end.

1. Make holes with a drawing pin on opposite sides of the rim of a plastic cup. Tie some string through the holes.

2. Make a hole in the bottom of the cup using a drawing pin. Push a ballpoint pen into the hole to widen it.

The petals should stick out from the base of the cup.

3. Push a small cotton wool ball into the hole, so half is inside the cup and half is poking out of the bottom.

4. Cut out petal shapes from colourful plastic bags. Glue them to the cup, around the cotton ball, to make a flower.

Don't stand too close or you may frighten the butterflies away.

5. Put nine tablespoons of water into a jug. Stir in a tablespoon of sugar. Pour the mixture into the cup.

6. Hang the feeder from a branch. Check on it from time to time during the day. Are any butterflies feeding?

What's going on?

Sugary water is similar to nectar, the sweet liquid that butterflies drink from flowers. The bright petals attract butterflies to the feeder. Then they can suck the sugary water as it soaks through the cotton wool ball.

A butterfly has a long tube called a proboscis to drink nectar from flowers.

Kaleidoscope

Discover how mirrors can be used to reflect light and create patterns.

1. Fold a postcard in half, so that the shorter edges meet. Then fold it in half the same way again. Open it out.

Clear plastic can be found in some packaging.

2. Find some clear, stiff plastic. Cut a piece the same size as the postcard and lay it on top of the postcard.

3. Score lines on the plastic, on top of the postcard folds, using scissors and a ruler. Put the plastic to one side.

4. Now cut out a piece of foil the same size as the postcard. Glue it onto the postcard and smooth it out with your fingers.

The foil and plastic are on the insides.

5. Lay the plastic on the foil and fold the postcard into a triangular tube. Tape the fourth flap over the first.

6. Cut out a piece of tracing paper larger than the end of the tube. Draw patterns on it using felt-tip pens.

7. Look through one end of the tube and hold the paper to the other end. Point it to the light and move the paper around.

What's going on?

Light shines through the decorated tracing paper into the tube. The plastic-covered foil sides act like mirrors, reflecting the light. Each side also reflects the light that reflects from the other sides. All these different reflections create interesting patterns of coloured light.

Be a snake charmer

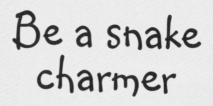

Experiment with static electricity in this charming activity.

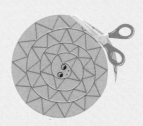

1. Put a plate on a piece of tissue paper and draw around it. Cut out the circle. Draw a spiral snake inside it, like this.

2. To decorate your snake, draw a zigzag pattern and eyes with felt-tip pens. Then cut along the spiral.

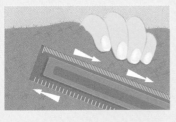

3. Rub a plastic ruler fairly hard and fast for half a minute with a scarf or sweater made of wool.

4. Then touch the snake's head with your ruler. Slowly lift the ruler. The snake should uncoil and rise up.

What's going on?

When the wool is rubbed against the plastic ruler, it causes particles too small to see to pass from the wool to the ruler. These extra particles on the ruler cause a build-up of static electricity. The static pulls on the tissue paper. The tissue paper is so light that the static on the ruler is strong enough to lift it.

As you rub the ruler, it gains extra particles.

The particles are transferred from the wool.

Balancing acrobats

A force called gravity will always pull you down to Earth. See it for yourself here.

Make the ball about the size of a table tennis ball.

1. Roll modelling clay between your palms to make a smooth ball. Cut it in half with a knife to make a base.

2. To make an acrobat, get a piece of card the size of a postcard. Draw a banana shape with a head.

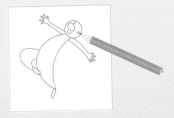

3. Draw outstretched arms and another small banana shape for a leg. Add hands, feet and a face.

You can decorate your acrobat using felt-tip pens.

Tab

4. Draw a square tab under the foot. Then cut around the outside of the acrobat, including the tab.

Be careful not to squash the base out of shape.

5. Make a slit in the top of the base with a knife, then slot the tab into it. Now try to push your acrobat over.

What's going on?

When you try to push over the acrobat, he pops back up. This is because the round base weighs more than the body. This uneven spread of weight affects how gravity pulls on things. The heavier the lower part of something is, the more easily it can stay upright.

Milk shapes

Mix vinegar and milk and get some surprising results.

1. Half fill a jar with milk, then pour it into a saucepan. Gently warm the milk on a hob, but don't let it boil.

2. Turn off the heat. Add a drop of food dye and two tablespoons of vinegar. Stir the milk until lumps form.

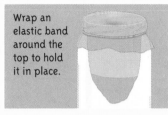

Wrap an elastic band around the top to hold it in place.

You'll be left with little lumps.

3. Cut a foot off a pair of tights. Put the toe inside the jar and fold the top over the sides, to make a strainer.

4. Pour the milk into the strainer and leave it for ten minutes. Squeeze out the rest of the milk into the jar.

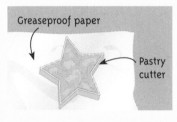

Greaseproof paper

Pastry cutter

The shape isn't edible!

5. Scoop the lumps out of the strainer and squeeze them into one lump. Press the lump into a pastry cutter.

6. Remove the cutter. Leave the shape on some paper. It will take a couple of days for it to dry.

What's going on?

Milk contains chains of molecules known as casein, which are normally curled up and dissolved. When you add vinegar, the molecules curl into a different shape and form solid plastic lumps instead.

Foaming monster

Watch a chemical reaction when you make this foaming monster.

1. Get a piece of thick paper, half the height of a small plastic bottle. Draw a monster's tail and cut it out.

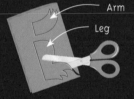

Arm

Leg

2. Fold another piece of paper in half. Draw an arm and a leg. Cut them out through both layers of paper.

You could make teeth from white paper.

3. Tape the tail to one side of the bottle. On the other side, tape the legs to the bottom and the arms above them.

4. Cut out two small circles from white paper. Draw a dot on each one. Glue them above the tail to make eyes.

5. Half fill the bottle with vinegar. Add a good squirt of washing-up liquid and a drop of food dye.

6. Gently swirl the bottle to mix the contents. Then place it in the middle of a large baking tray or dish.

7. Put a heaped teaspoon of bicarbonate of soda in the middle of a square of tissue. Roll it up and twist the ends.

8. Drop the tissue into the bottle. After a couple of minutes, foam will come out of the monster's mouth.

What's going on?

When you mix vinegar and bicarbonate of soda, it makes a gas called carbon dioxide. This forms bubbles in the vinegar. The bubbles of gas react with the washing-up liquid to make foam. The whole combination reacts so much that foam pours out of the monster's mouth.

Fire a balloon rocket

Fire a balloon rocket and see
how forces do their job.

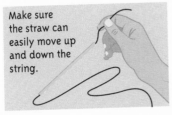

Make sure the straw can easily move up and down the string.

1. Cut a piece of string, about 3m (10ft) long, and thread it through a straw. Tie one end to a dining chair.

2. Tie the other end of the string to another chair. Pull the chairs apart to make the string tight.

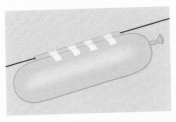

3. Blow up a balloon and hold the neck closed with a paperclip. Tape the balloon to the straw, like this.

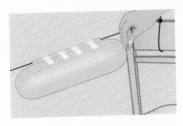

4. Push the balloon to one end of the string, with the neck facing a chair. Take the paperclip off. What happens?

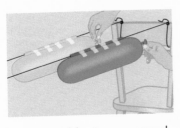

5. You could set up a second line and attach another balloon. Now you can race them with a friend.

What's going on?

As the balloon deflates, it pushes out the air inside the balloon. The air pushes the balloon away from the chair and along the string in the opposite direction. Scientists describe this with a rule: every action has an equal and opposite reaction.

Sinking diver

Watch air under pressure in this activity.

1. Find a piece of paper that will fit halfway round a big plastic bottle. Draw an underwater scene on it and tape it around the bottle, so you can see it from the front.

2. Find a pen lid with a pocket clip, and attach a paperclip, like this. If there is a hole in the top of the lid, block it with a little poster tack.

3. Cut out a diver shape from thin, coloured plastic. Then press the diver on to the paperclip with poster tack.

The diver must be narrow enough to fit through the neck of the bottle.

5. Fill the bottle with water. Then carefully lower the diver through the neck and screw the lid on.

4. Put the diver in a tall glass of water. The model should float near the top. If it's too heavy and sinks, remove some of the poster tack.

6. Squeeze the sides of the bottle and the diver will sink. Then let go, and the diver will float up to the surface again.

The diver will move slowly at first, so watch carefully.

What's going on?

An air bubble is trapped in the pen top when you drop the diver in. Squeezing the bottle pushes water up the top which squashes the air bubble and lets water in, making the diver sink. When you stop squeezing, the air bubble returns to normal size, pushing the water out. So the diver floats again.

Seeing DNA

Watch DNA emerge in front of your eyes.

Special equipment

You can get surgical spirit from pharmacies.

1. Finely chop an onion and put the pieces in a bowl. Mix in enough washing-up liquid to coat but not cover them.

2. Then add half a teaspoon of salt and two tablespoons of water. Stir gently to avoid making foam or bubbles.

3. Leave the mixture for ten minutes. Then stir it again and use a sieve to strain off the liquid into another bowl.

Remember to put the lid back on the surgical spirit.

4. Pour the liquid into a glass jar. Use a spoon to scrape off any foam or bubbles from the surface.

5. Pour surgical spirit gently down the inside of the jar. The spirit will form a separate layer. Don't stir the layers.

6. After about 20 minutes, a stringy white substance will appear in the top layer. This is the onion's DNA.

What's going on?

The salt and washing-up liquid help to break down the onion's cells, releasing the DNA. DNA doesn't dissolve in alcohol-based liquids such as surgical spirit. So it appears as the solid, white strands that you see floating in the surgical spirit on top of the washing-up liquid.

Paper planes

Find out how the shape of the wing can change a plane's direction.

1. Fold a piece of A4 paper in half so that the long sides meet. Open it out and fold the top corners to the crease.

2. Fold down the whole triangle shape you've just made, so that the tip lines up with the crease in the middle.

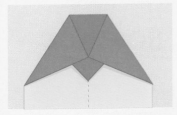

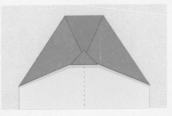

3. Then fold down the corners at the top so that they meet a little way above the tip of the triangle, like this.

4. Now fold up the tip of the triangle, so that it overlaps the folded-down flaps and holds them in place.

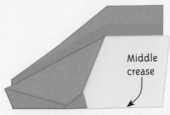

Middle crease

5. Turn the paper over. Then fold it in half down the middle crease and smooth out the creases.

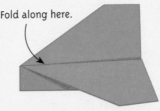

Fold along here.

6. To make wings, fold both sides down at the point shown here. Throw the plane to see how well it flies.

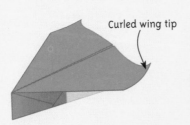

Curled wing tip

7. Curl the corner tips of the wings up or down around a pencil. How does this affect the plane's flight?

What's going on?

The fronts of the wings are thickest, which helps the plane to fly. Curling the wing tips changes the air flow. Curling up the left tip makes the plane steer to the left and vice versa. Curling up both tips makes the plane climb. Curling them down makes the plane dive.

Meringue science

Why are meringues foamy and light? Find out here.

If the yolk breaks up, you will need to start again with a new egg.

1. Cut a piece of baking parchment to fit inside a baking tray. Heat the oven to 110°C (225°F, gas mark ¼).

2. Crack an egg on the edge of a bowl. Gently pull the shell apart and tip the white and yolk onto a saucer.

You won't need the yolk.

Use an electric whisk if you can; it's quicker!

3. Hold a small cup over the yolk and tip the saucer so that the egg white dribbles into the bowl.

4. Beat the egg white. After about 15 minutes, it forms a thick foam and the whisk makes peaks when you lift it.

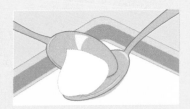

5. Add 50g (2oz) of caster sugar, a teaspoonful at a time. Whisk the mixture after adding each spoonful.

6. Take a heaped teaspoon of the mixture and slide it onto the baking parchment using another teaspoon.

Use oven gloves.

7. Do the same again, leaving gaps between each spoonful. Put the tray in the oven to bake for 45 minutes.

8. Turn off the oven and leave the meringues in for 15 more minutes. Then take them out and leave them to cool.

What's going on?

Egg white contains chains called albumin. Whisking whips air bubbles into the egg. The albumin traps the bubbles, making a foam. When you bake it, the foam hardens into meringues.

Before whisking, the albumin chains are quite tightly curled up.

After whisking, the chains uncurl and form a net that traps the air bubbles.

Air bubble

Making butter

Make your own butter and find
out about the science behind it.

It's tiring, so you may want a friend to help you shake!

1. Half fill a clean jar with double cream. Add a pinch of salt for taste. Screw the lid on tightly and shake the jar.

2. Shake the jar for about 10-15 minutes. Eventually, it will separate into a lump of fat and a milky liquid.

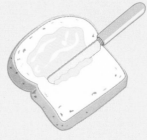

3. Take out the lump and put it on a paper towel. Wrap the towel around it and squeeze out any excess liquid.

4. Now taste it. The lump you have made is butter. Put it in a dish, keep it in the fridge, and spread it on some bread.

What's going on?

Cream is a mixture of tiny blobs of fat spread evenly through a milky liquid. When you shake the cream, the tiny blobs of fat bump into each other. The more you shake, the more they bump and join together. Eventually they turn into butter.

65

Fruity ice slush

Make your own delicious slush drink,
without a fridge!

Don't let salty ice get in the glass.

1. Fill a mixing bowl with ice cubes. Sprinkle three tablespoons of salt on top of the ice cubes and stir it in.

2. Carefully place a glass upright in the middle of the ice. Half fill the glass with fruit juice.

If it's a hot day, you may need to add more ice.

3. Stir the juice every 10 minutes with a spoon. After about an hour and a half, the juice will become slushy.

4. Stir it every 5 minutes for another half hour until it becomes slush. Then you can eat it or leave it to freeze solid.

What's going on?

Adding salt makes the ice melt at a lower temperature. In the bowl you get very cold salty ice and water. This mixture absorbs heat from the fruit juice, making the juice colder and colder. Eventually it will freeze solid, but stirring it breaks up the ice, so that it forms a slush instead.

Floating flowers

Float these flowers in water and
watch what happens.

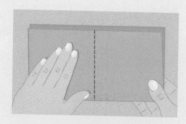

1. Cut out a square of paper
about 15cm x 15cm (6in x
6in). Fold it in half one way
and then in half again.

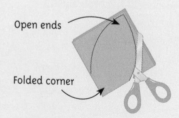

Open ends

Folded corner

2. Draw a petal shape
outwards from the folded
corner. Cut around the shape
to make the petals.

3. Open out the paper. Fold the tip of each petal to the middle point — the place where the creases cross.

4. To make a beetle to hide in the flower, draw an oval body on bright paper, add six legs and cut it out.

5. Cut out two wing shapes and two eyes in different-coloured paper and glue them onto the body.

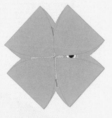

6. Put the beetle inside the flower. Fold down the petals. Fill a sink with water and lay it on top. What happens?

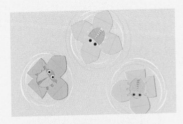

7. You could make more flowers from different types of paper. Do some open faster than others?

What's going on?

As the fibres in the paper soak up water, they swell and the paper expands. As this happens there is a slight movement which makes the flower open up. Different types of paper soak up water at different speeds.

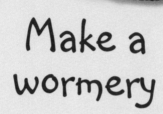

Make a wormery

See how worms' wriggling techniques mix up the soil and help plants grow.

1. Make a hole with a drawing pin at the top of a large plastic bottle. Then cut the top off, like this.

If you don't have sand, try to find different colours of soil.

2. Fill the bottle with layers of soil and thinner layers of sand. Put dead leaves and four teaspoons of water on top.

You can often find worms under piles of dead leaves.

3. Dig around in some soil until you find two or three earthworms. Carefully put them into your bottle.

4. Cover the top of the bottle with food wrap and poke air holes in it with a pencil. Tape dark paper around the sides.

The paper has been taken off.

5. Add a couple of teaspoons of water each day, to keep the soil damp. After two weeks, take the paper off.

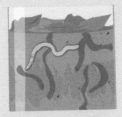

6. The worms will have mixed up the soil and made tunnels. Now return the worms to their original home.

What's going on?

Worms mix everything up as they make their burrows. The different-coloured layers of soil and sand make it easier for you to see how they do this. It's great for gardens, as the mixing adds air to the soil and the burrows make channels for water. The worms may have pulled the dead leaves down to eat. This mixes nutrients into the soil. All this helps plants get everything they need from the soil to grow healthily.

Team trail

See how ants can organise
some clever teamwork.

If the ant ignores the fruit, move it in front of it again.

1. First you need some ants. You may have to wait until the summer to find them on paths around your home.

2. When you have found an ant, put a thin slice of fruit in front of it. It may eat some of it or carry bits away.

One ant may attract more ants, until they make a trail.

3. Check the fruit after an hour. Have other ants been attracted to it? If so, what are they doing?

4. When there are lots of ants, move the fruit to a new position, a little to the side. What do the ants do?

What's going on?

You can see one of the best examples of insect teamwork by watching ants. If one ant finds food, it leads others there to eat it too. They follow each other by making long trails. The ants go back and forth collecting food, to take back to their nest. When you move the fruit, the ants will still find it. But, instead of making a new direct route to the food, they will follow each other via their old trail route.

Speedy shoots

Grow your own plants from dried seeds.

You could use chickpeas or any dried beans, such as broad beans or kidney beans.

1. Take two glasses of water. Put four lemon pips in one and four beans in the other. Leave them to soak for a day.

2. Stuff two jars with paper towels or napkins. Pour water into each one until the towels are soaked through.

You should be able to see the seeds through the jars.

3. Drain the seeds. Push the beans down the sides of one jar, and the lemon seeds down the sides of the other.

4. Put the jars in a warm, dark cupboard. Check them each day and add water, if needed, to keep them wet.

The beans should sprout after a few days. The lemon seeds will take longer.

The new pots give the plants space to grow.

5. Once the beans and seeds sprout, move the jars to a light place, such as a windowsill. Keep them wet.

6. They will grow roots. After a week or two, plant them, root down, in small pots of soil, and water regularly.

What's going on?

Putting the seeds in a dark cupboard encourages them to seek light and sprout. Once they've sprouted, light and water are essential for them to grow successfully. Beans and chickpeas sprout quickly. Most bean plants will grow and die in a year. Lemon trees live and grow for years, but their seeds may take several weeks before they sprout.

Indicator paper

You can use red cabbage to make your own acid and alkali testers.

Chop the cabbage into small pieces.

Special equipment
You can buy blotting paper from most stationery shops.

1. Chop up half a red cabbage. Put it in a saucepan. Cover it with water and bring it to the boil. Then leave it to cool.

Red cabbage juice stains. Don't get it on your clothes or furniture.

2. Rest a sieve on top of a big bowl and pour the cabbage mixture into it. Leave the drained liquid to cool.

These will be your indicator paper strips.

3. Cut finger-sized strips from blotting paper or thick paper towels. Dip them in the liquid and leave them to dry.

4. Pour about 1cm (½in) of vinegar into a cup. Then pour 1cm (½in) of water into another cup.

5. In a third cup, stir in half a teaspoon of bicarbonate of soda to 1cm (½in) of water.

6. Dip a dry indicator strip into the cup of vinegar. What happens to the indicator paper?

7. Now test another strip in the water and one in the bicarbonate of soda liquid. Does the same thing happen?

What's going on?

The indicator papers change colour when you mix them with an acid or an alkali. Acids always turn the paper red and alkalis always turn it green. So you can use the paper as an acid and alkali detector. Vinegar is an acid and bicarbonate of soda is an alkali. Water is neutral — it's neither acid nor alkali — so doesn't make the paper change colour.

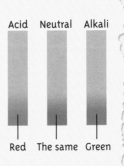

Acid   Neutral   Alkali

Red   The same   Green

Surface tension

Create beautiful patterns while
experimenting with surface tension.

1. Half fill a small bowl with water. Then sprinkle a thin layer of ground pepper on the surface.

2. Dip a cocktail stick in washing-up liquid. Then touch the middle of the water with the stick's tip.

3. As the washing-up liquid touches the water, watch the grains of pepper. What happens to them?

Use several colours of food dye if you have them.

4. Half fill another small bowl with milk. Then add two or three drops of food dye in different places.

You can touch the milk in several places to make the dyes blend more.

5. Dip a cocktail stick in washing-up liquid and touch the milk with it. What happens to the dyes as you do this?

What's going on?

Washing-up liquid reduces surface tension. This allows the particles of water at the surface to spread out more. As they spread out, they push the pepper specks or the food dyes, so that they spread out and merge together, creating patterns.

79

Flick book

Try this eye-catching activity to
see how movies are made.

1. You need a small pad of paper, thin enough to see through for tracing. Draw a stick man on the last page.

You can see the first picture through the page.

2. Turn to the second to last page. Trace the outline of the man, but slightly change the position of an arm or leg.

This stick man is kicking his leg.

3. Keep tracing the picture from the page below, but make small changes each time as if the man has moved.

4. Draw at least 20 pictures like this. Flick through them from back to front. Your stick man will appear to move.

What's going on?

As you flick the pages, your eyes and brain try to blend the pictures together, so the stick man seems to move. Movies need to show 24 pictures every second to make the image smooth enough to look as if it's really moving.

In movies, the pictures are joined together in a long strip, so that they can quickly pass through the projector.

Bottle flute

Find out how blowing into bottles
can make musical notes.

1. Pour different amounts of water into a selection of glass bottles. Don't fill any to the top.

2. Rest the neck of one bottle on your lower lip. Blow gently across the top until you hear a note.

If you can't get a note, change the angle, or how hard you blow.

3. Blow gently across all the bottles in turn. Do different levels of water make different notes?

4. You could add food dye to the water, so that you can see the levels more easily.

What's going on?

Blowing makes the air inside the bottle vibrate, producing a note. The notes change according to the amount of water and air in the bottle. The bigger the space between the water and the top of the bottle, the lower the note.

Spider slider

See the gripping force, known as friction, at work in this experiment.

1. Snip the head off a used match. Then cut out a piece of card two match lengths long and one wide.

2. Press the match into some poster tack across the middle of the strip. Then fold up each end of the strip.

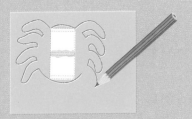

3. Draw a spider shape on bright paper. Make sure the spider is bigger than the strip of card.

4. Cut out the spider shape. Make eyes and fangs from more paper. Glue them on to give the spider a face.

Remove the needle when the thread is through the holes.

5. Glue the card onto the back of the spider, like this. Then cut a piece of cotton thread as long as your arm.

6. Thread a needle with the cotton and thread it through the middle of the two folds of the card strip.

7. Hold the thread tight between your hands, with one hand above the other. Let the thread go slack. What happens?

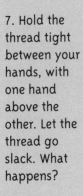

What's going on?

When the thread is held taut, it touches the match. This causes friction between the match and the thread, which is strong enough to stop the spider from moving down the thread. But, when you let the thread go slack, it no longer touches the match. This means there is less friction, so the spider slides down easily.

Words and pictures

Discover how your brain is
influenced by words and pictures.

dog bee mouse cat

bat frog squirrel dinosaur

goldfish seal cockerel elephant

dolphin lion crocodile butterfly

1. Look at the pictures above and say the name of
the animal out loud. Do not read the word.

2. Now look at the pictures below. Say the names of the animals out loud. Is it harder?

crocodile bat cockerel frog

dolphin mouse lion cat

dinosaur goldfish butterfly bee

elephant seal squirrel dog

What's going on?

The first pictures are easy to name because the word below them is the same as the picture. The second group of pictures is harder because of the interference of different information. Most people can read quicker than they can name a picture. The different animal word below the picture confuses your brain.

Tricky pictures

Trick your eyes with these
strange illusions.

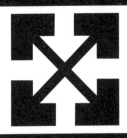

1. Is the red spot at the back or front of the box? Can you get it to switch places just by staring for a long time?

2. What do you see in the picture above? Do you see two people looking at each other — or an ornate vase?

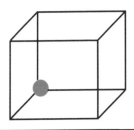

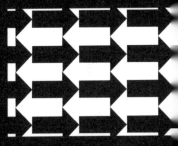

3. Do you see four arrows pointing into the middle of the square, or four arrows pointing to the corners?

4. Which way are the arrows pointing? Do you see white arrows pointing left or black ones pointing right?

What's going on?

Your brain can flick between two ways of looking at each of these pictures. This is because the pictures lack the extra details and shading that would normally help your brain to figure out which view is the right one.

Name that face

Do you find it difficult to remember people's names? Try this and improve your memory.

Choose people you don't know.

David   Helen

1. Cut out eight different faces from magazines. Glue them onto pieces of card and turn them face down.

2. Write a name on the back of each card. Read out the name and then look at the face. Try to learn the names.

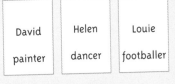

David	Helen	Louie
painter	dancer	footballer

3. Mix up the cards. Then go through them just looking at the faces. Can you remember the names?

4. Now add a different hobby below each name. Mix them up and try to remember them. Is it easier?

What's going on?

It's hard to remember names by themselves, as there are no other clues to help your memory. But adding extra information, such as hobbies, helps your brain form links so that you remember the name. Going through the names a second time also helps you remember.

Pinhole projector

Try this experiment and see
the world upside down.

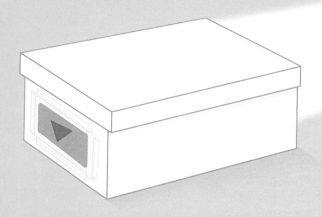

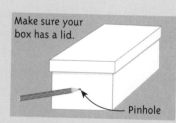

Make sure your
box has a lid.

Pinhole

1. Push a drawing pin into
the middle of one end of a
shoe box to make a hole.
Push a pencil in to widen it.

This is the
viewer.

2. Cut out a rectangular
window at the other end of
the box. Tape greaseproof
paper over it.

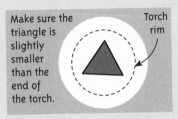

Make sure the triangle is slightly smaller than the end of the torch.

Torch rim

3. Cut another piece of greaseproof paper big enough to cover the lightbulb end of a torch.

4. Draw a triangle on the paper. Use felt-tip pens to fill the triangle in dark green or blue and outline it in black.

The image will be blurry.

5. Tape the paper to the end of the torch. Switch on the torch and place it on a surface in a dark room.

6. Stand 1m (3ft) from the torch. Look through the viewer, pointing the pinhole at the light. What do you see?

What's going on?

Light from the torch passes through the pinhole onto your viewer. Light rays from the top of the torch hit the bottom of the viewer, and rays from the bottom hit the top. These rays cross over when they pass through the pinhole, so you see the triangle upside down.

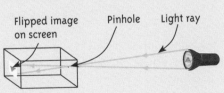

Flipped image on screen   Pinhole   Light ray

What grows best?

Find out what seeds need
to grow well.

1. Take three plates and make
a pile of ten kitchen towels
on each one. Lay a pastry
cutter on each pile.

2. Spoon water onto two of
the plates to soak the towels.
Write "dry" along one side
of the pile without water.

3. Sprinkle cress seeds into each cutter. Hold the cutter and spread the seeds to the edges with your finger.

4. Carefully remove the cutters. Put one of the watered plates in a cupboard, and the other two near a window.

The cress plants should grow in the shape of the cutters.

5. Every day, add water around the seeds on the "wet" plates, but don't pour water over the seeds.

6. After about a week, some of the seeds will have grown into plants. Which plates look the healthiest?

What's going on?

The dry seeds don't grow at all, as seeds need water to sprout. But, once they've sprouted, they need light to make food, so the plants in the dark cupboard are yellow. The wet plate by the window grows successfully, as it has both water and light.

Wind vane

Watch the weather change with this breezy activity.

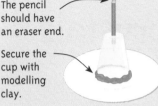

The pencil should have an eraser end.

Secure the cup with modelling clay.

1. Make a hole in the top of a plastic cup with a drawing pin. Push a pencil through it. Secure the cup to a plate.

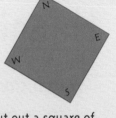

2. Cut out a square of coloured card and mark the corners, North, South, East and West, like this.

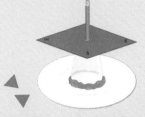

3. Cut a hole in the middle of the card and push it over the pencil. Then cut two small triangles from card.

The triangles should point, like this.

4. Tape the triangles to the ends of a straw. Push a pin through the middle of the straw and then into the eraser.

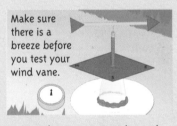

Make sure there is a breeze before you test your wind vane.

5. Put the vane outside and point it so that N matches North on a compass. Which way does the wind turn it?

What's going on?

The wind blows on the wind vane and turns it until the arrows point in the direction the wind is coming from. The direction of the wind helps weather forecasters predict changes in the weather.

Hanging crystals

Watch these amazing crystals
grow on a piece of wool.

Be careful when pouring
very hot water.

When a layer forms at the bottom, it means no more will dissolve.

1. Fill two jars with hot water. Stir in about six teaspoons of bicarbonate of soda, until no more will dissolve.

2. Put the jars in a warm place where they won't get moved, with a small plate in between them.

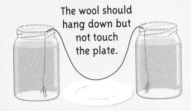

The wool should hang down but not touch the plate.

3. Cut a piece of wool as long as your arm. Tie a paperclip to each end of it and place one end in each jar.

4. Leave the jars for a week. Crystals will grow along the wool and hang down over the plate.

What's going on?

The wool soaks up the mixture. When the water evaporates, all that's left are bicarbonate of soda crystals. The hanging crystals are formed when the mixture starts to drip from the wool and evaporate. If you're lucky, you might even get crystals that drip onto the plate and form columns.

Paper compass

The Earth contains iron. Explore how this affects magnetism.

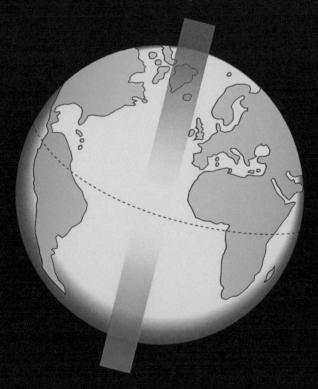

Special equipment

You can buy strong magnets from toy or hardware stores. Don't use fridge magnets, as they're too weak.

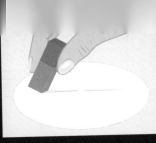

1. Draw around a glass on a piece of thin paper. Cut out the circle. Then thread a big needle through it, like this.

2. Stroke the needle 20 times in the same direction with one end of a magnet. Lift the magnet between strokes.

Be patient; it may take a moment before it moves.

You can check this with a real compass.

3. Fill a bowl with water and float the paper on top. After a moment, it will slowly spin around and then stop.

4. If you turn the paper now, the needle will still spin back to point the same way. It will be facing north-south.

What's going on?

A needle is made of steel, which contains particles of iron, jumbled up. But when you stroke a needle with a magnet, the iron particles become temporarily magnetized. Inside the Earth there is so much iron that it acts like a giant magnet, giving the Earth a magnetic field. The magnetized needle lines up with the Earth's magnetic field. This makes it act like a compass, so it always turns to point north-south.

Jumbled iron particles in a needle

Ordered iron particles in a magnetized needle

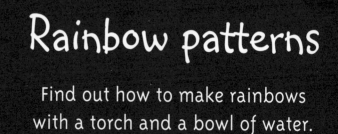

Rainbow patterns

Find out how to make rainbows
with a torch and a bowl of water.

Make rainbow paper

1. Half fill a bowl with water. Add one drop of clear nail varnish to the surface of the water. It will spread out.

2. Dip a small piece of black paper into the water and lift it out. Let it dry. If you tilt the paper you will see rainbows.

Rainbow reflected

You may need to prop up the mirror with a small stone to keep it in place.

1. Fill a tub with water. Lean a small mirror at an angle at one end. Shine a torch onto the underwater part of the mirror.

2. Then hold a sheet of paper a little way behind the torch. Move it around until you can see a rainbow on the paper.

What's going on?

In the first activity, the varnish forms a thin layer on the water. When the varnish is transferred to the paper and light shines on it, the light is reflected by the layers of varnish. This creates rainbow patterns.

In the second activity, when a beam of light passes through water, the water makes the light bend. The different colours in light bend by different amounts, which makes them separate, making a rainbow. The mirror reflects the rainbow onto the paper.

Quacking duck vibrations

Experiment with vibrations to make a strangely familiar sound.

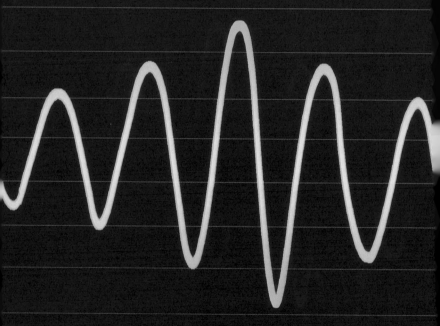

1. Make a hole in the bottom of a plastic cup using a drawing pin. Push a pencil into the hole to widen it.

2. Cut a piece of string that is about as long as your arm. Then make a couple of knots in one end of the string.

3. Thread the string through the hole, so that the knots rest on the outside of the bottom of the cup, like this.

4. Wet a paper towel. Hold the cup in one hand and drag the wet towel down the string with the other. What happens?

What's going on?

As you drag the wet paper towel along the string, it makes the string vibrate. The vibrating string makes the cup vibrate too, which makes the sound louder. The vibrations are uneven, so they make an unmusical sound rather like a quacking duck.

Salt and candy crystals

Make your own crystals in this dazzling activity.

Salt crystals

You can buy epsom salts from most pharmacies.

A dark plate will show the crystals more clearly. Don't eat them.

1. Half fill a mug with hot water. Gradually stir in about two tablespoons of epsom salts, until they are dissolved.

2. Pour two tablespoons of the liquid onto a small plate. Crystals will form after a couple of days.

Candy crystals

1. Half fill a mug with hot water. Gradually stir in about two tablespoons of sugar until it is dissolved.

2. Cover two small plates with tin foil and pour two tablespoons of the liquid onto each plate.

You can eat them!

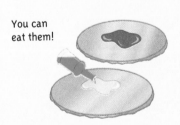

3. Add a different drop of food dye to each. Leave them in a warm room. After three days, crystals will form.

What's going on?

The water from the plates evaporates into the air and turns into water vapour — tiny water particles, spread so far apart that they are like a gas. Leaving the plates in a warm room speeds up the evaporation. Once the water has evaporated, only the crystals are left.

Index

acids, 76-77

air, 23, 55, 63, 83

    pressure, 56-57

alkalis, 76-77

balance, 48-49

brain, 11, 81, 86-87, 89, 91

bugs, 30-31

cells, 59

chemicals, 19, 52

chrysalis, 17

colours, 18-19, 76-77, 103

crystals, 98-99, 106-107

DNA, 58-59

Earth, 33, 48, 100-101

elastic, 38-39, 40-41

electricity, 15, 27

energy, 14-15, 26-27, 40-41

evaporation, 99, 107
eyes, 80-81, 88

fibres, 69
forces, 35, 54
    pull, 29, 35, 48-49, 55
    push, 48, 55
freezing, 67

generators, 15, 27

heat, 67
hydro-electric power
    stations, 27

ice, 67
illusions, 88
indicator paper, 77
iron, 29

light, 13, 44-45, 93, 103
liquids, 21, 37, 79

magnetism, 28-29, 100-101

melting, 67

metals, 29

mirrors, 44-45, 103

mixtures, 19, 21, 36-37, 65

music, 38, 82

nutrients, 71

particles, 21, 47, 79, 101, 107

plants, 17, 70-71, 74-75, 94-95

plastic, 33, 47, 51

power, 14, 26-27

pressure, 56

rainbows, 102-103

reflections, 44-45

roots, 75

salt, 67

seeds, 74-75, 94-95

shadows, 8-9

soil, 30-31, 70-71
solids, 21, 67
sound, 22-23, 39
static electricity, 32-33, 46-47
steel, 29, 101
sunlight, 12-13
surface tension, 78-79

temperature, 67

vapour, 107
vibration, 22-23, 39

water, 21, 26-27, 56-57, 67, 68-69, 79, 83, 102-103
weather, 96-97
weight, 25, 49
wind, 14-15, 96-97
wings, 60-61

Additional designs by Michelle Lawrence

This edition published in 2014 by Usborne Publishing Ltd, 83-85 Saffron Hill, London, EC1N 8RT, England.

www.usborne.com Copyright © 2014, 2008, 2005 Usborne Publishing Ltd.